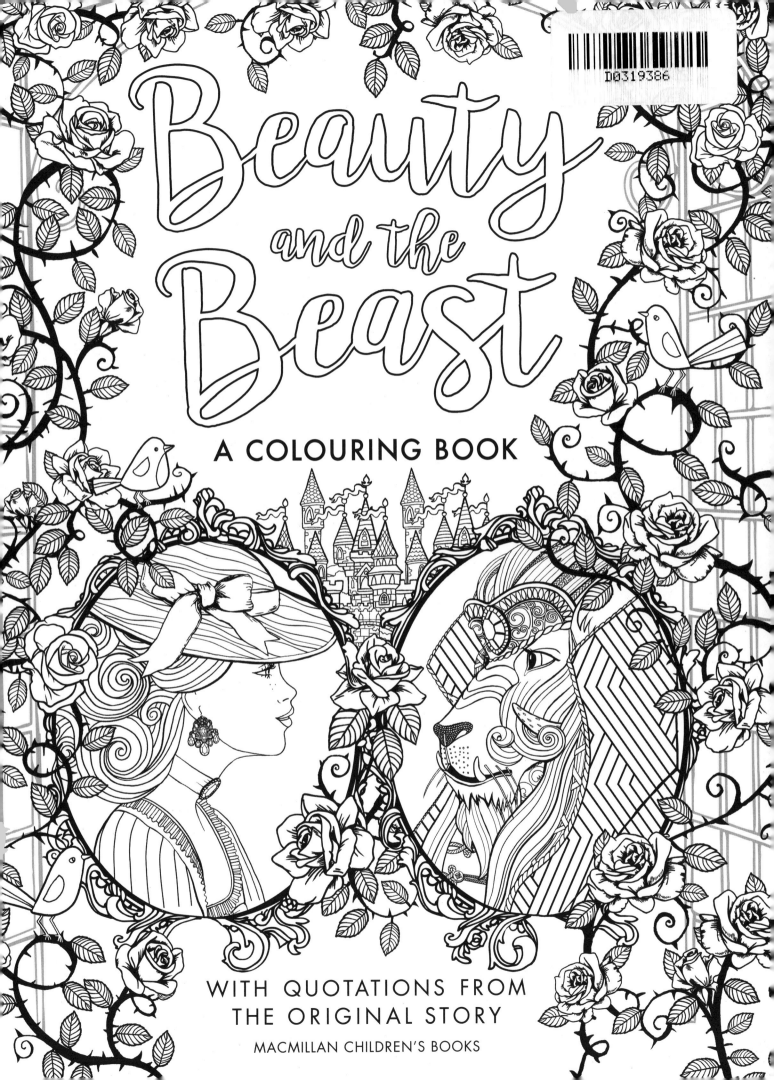

Beauty and the Beast

A COLOURING BOOK

WITH QUOTATIONS FROM
THE ORIGINAL STORY

MACMILLAN CHILDREN'S BOOKS

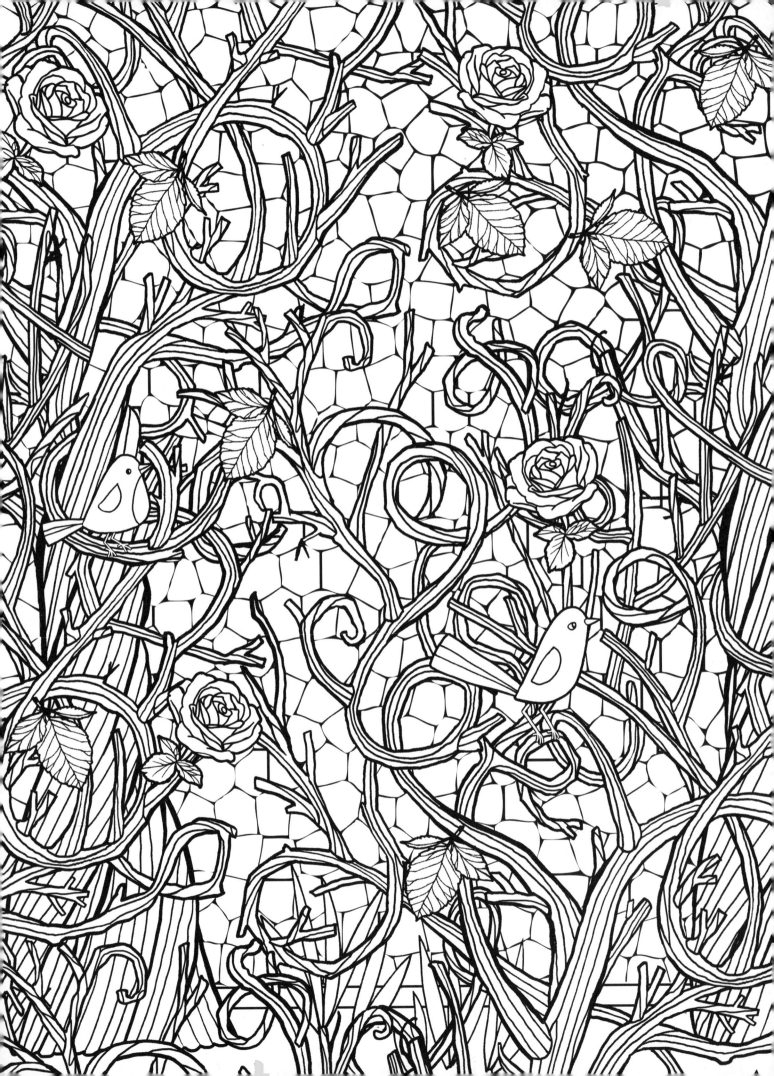

Going
through a **thick**
forest he suddenly
saw a light
— it came from a
palace lit from top
to bottom.

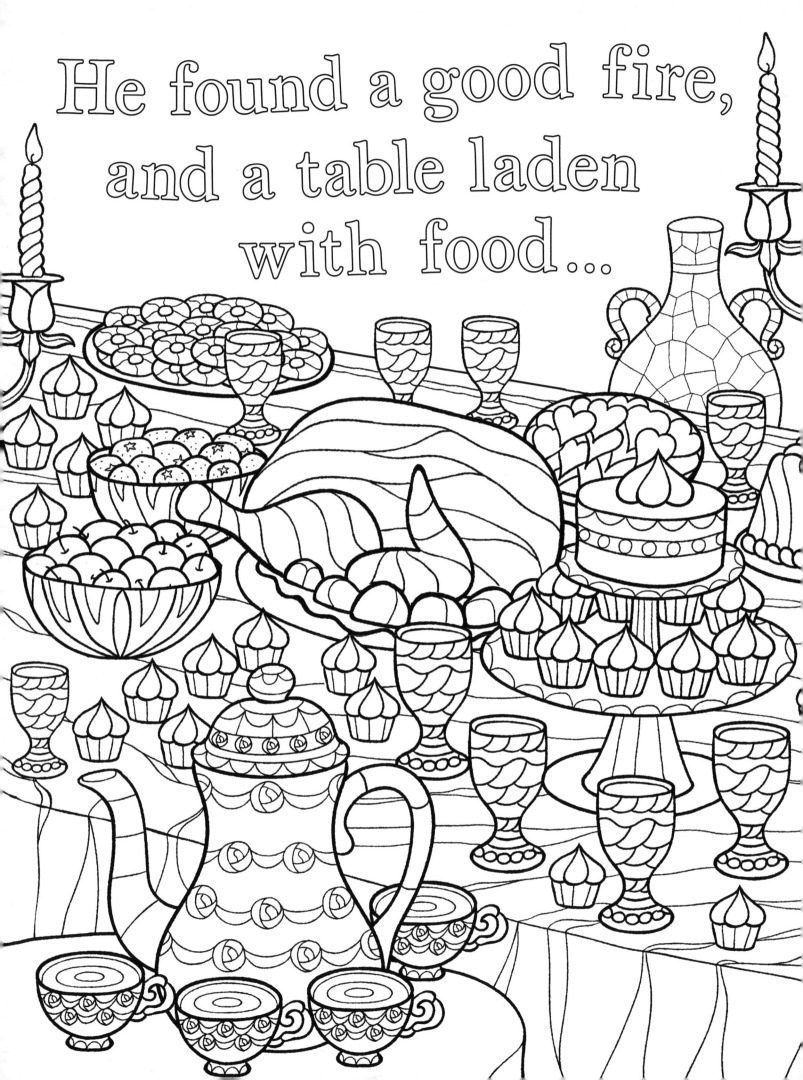

He found a good fire, and a table laden with food...

"You are very *ungrateful*," said the Beast in a terrible voice. "I saved your life, and in return you steal my roses."

Beauty insisted on setting out for the fine palace...

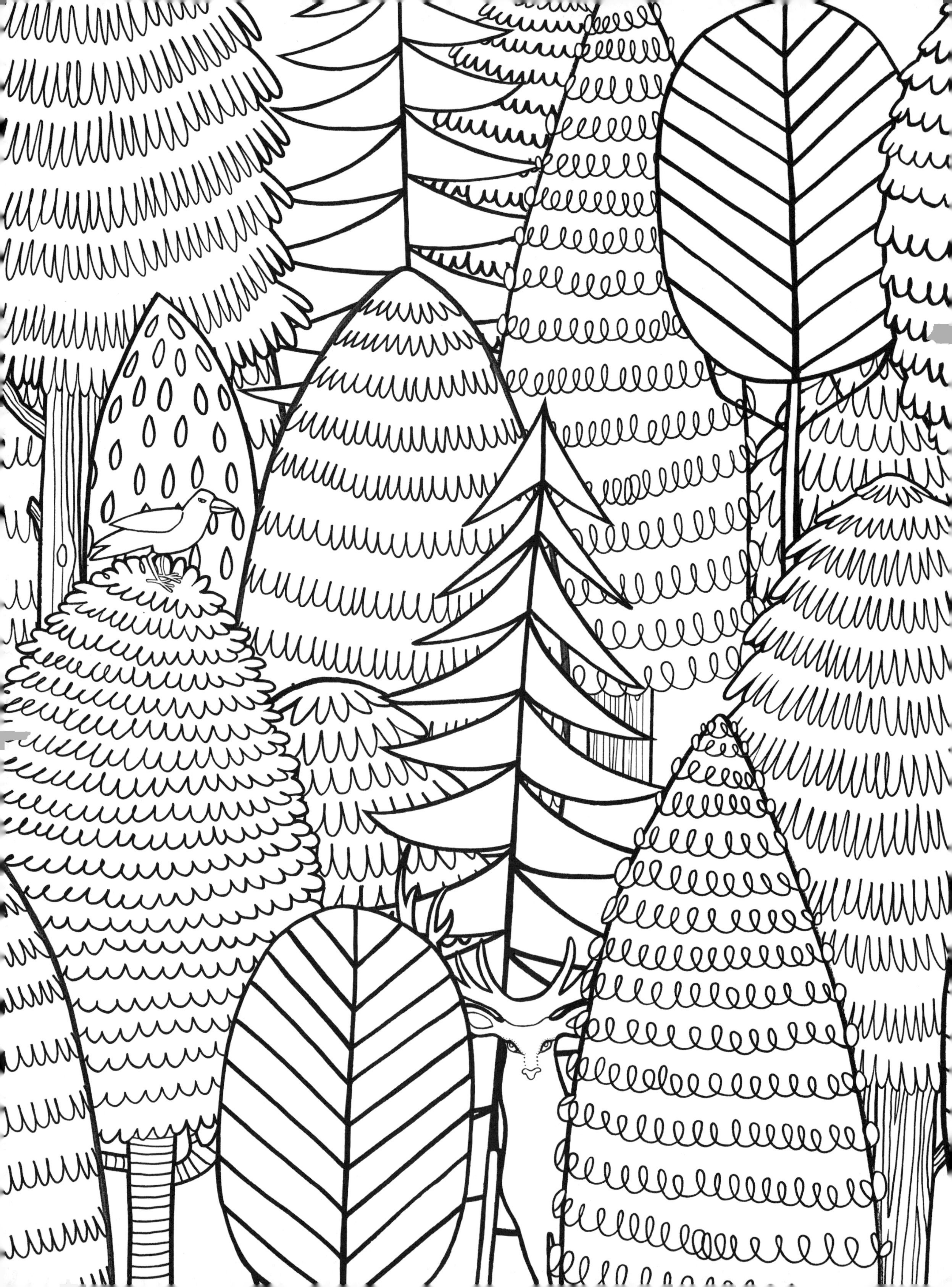

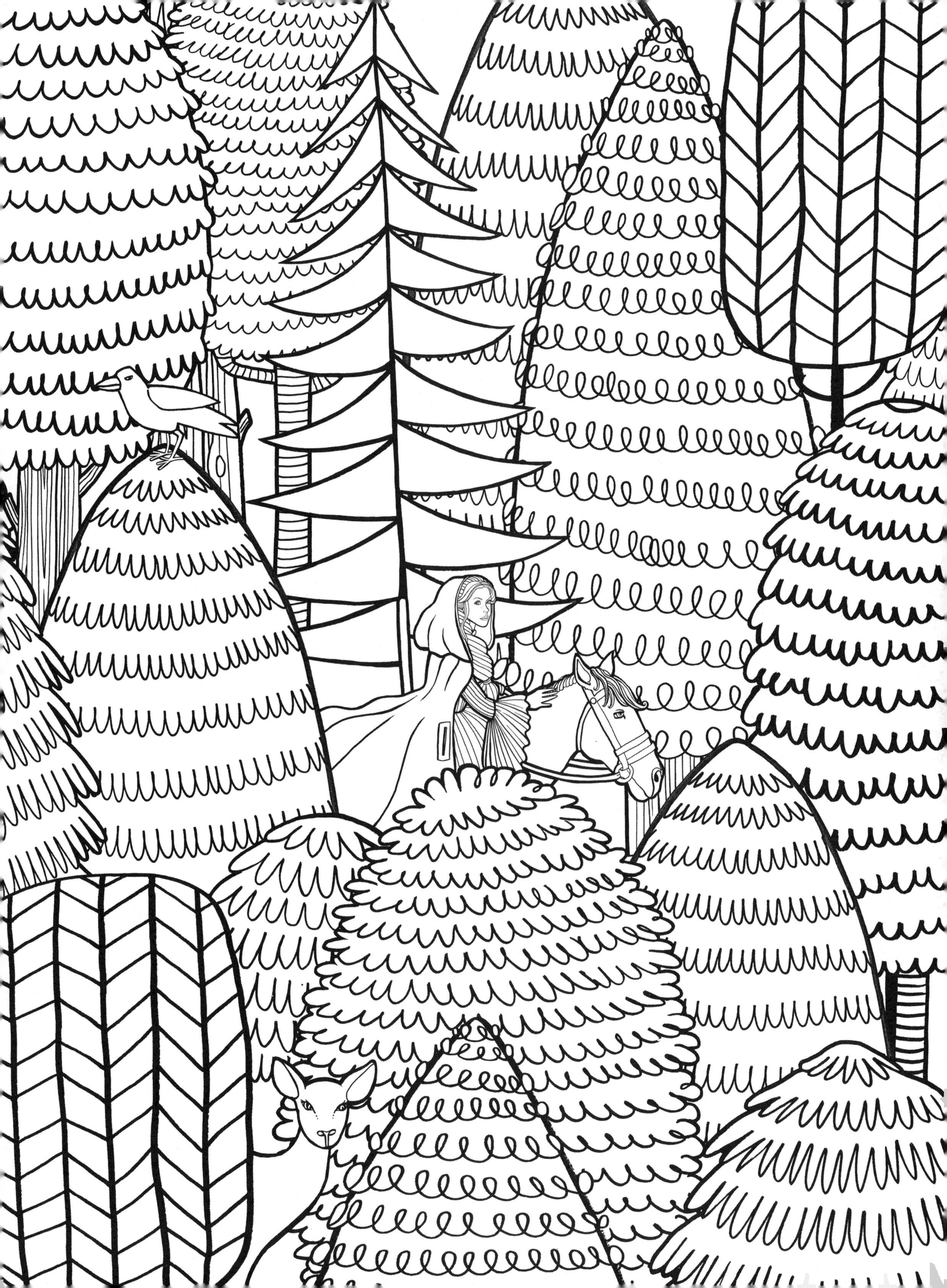

"*Beast,
I wish I could
consent to marry
you, but I cannot;
I shall always
love you as my
friend, try
to be happy
with this.*"

"My heart is good, but I am still a monster..."

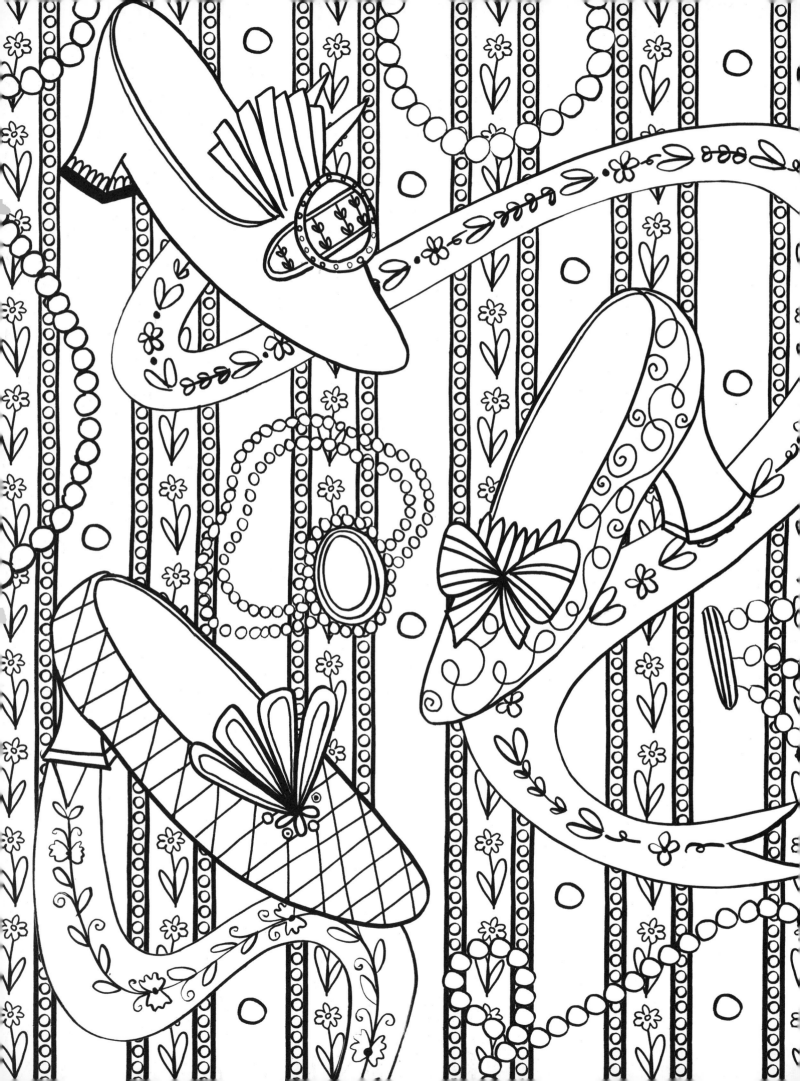

It was a
    beautiful room,
filled with
wonderful things.

Beauty found a little sewing room filled with pretty ribbons, buttons and silken threads for her use.

This morning
she decided to amuse
herself in the garden for
the sun was shining.

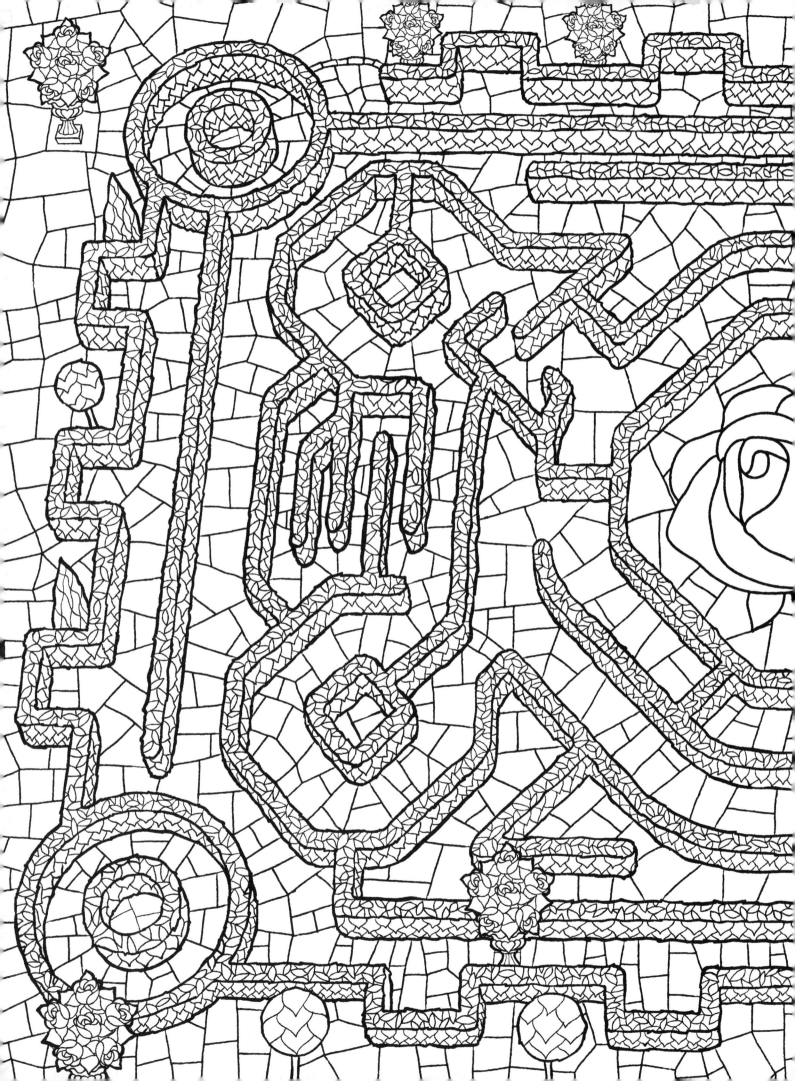

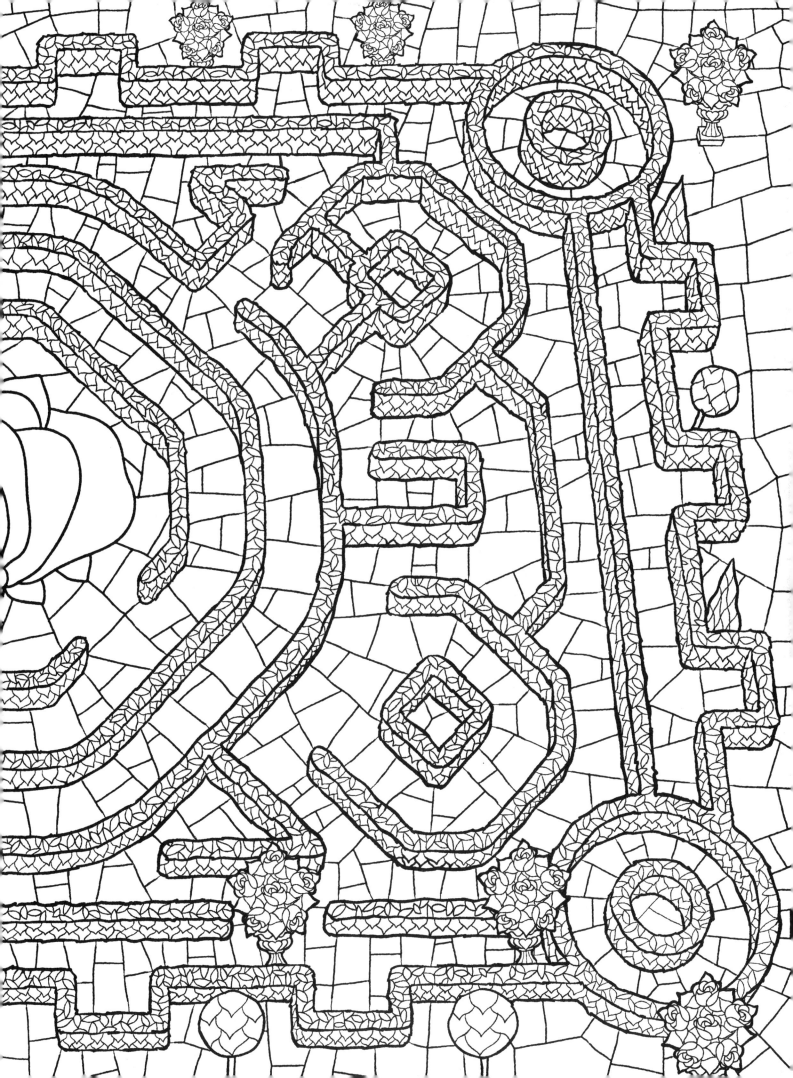

Out in
the gardens,
Beauty
found an
arbour covered
with the
prettiest
pink
roses.

Beauty had stopped being afraid of him. Now she knew that he was really gentle in spite of his ferocious looks and his dreadful voice.

"*Only you, Beauty,* had the heart to love me, and for that I shall love you forever."

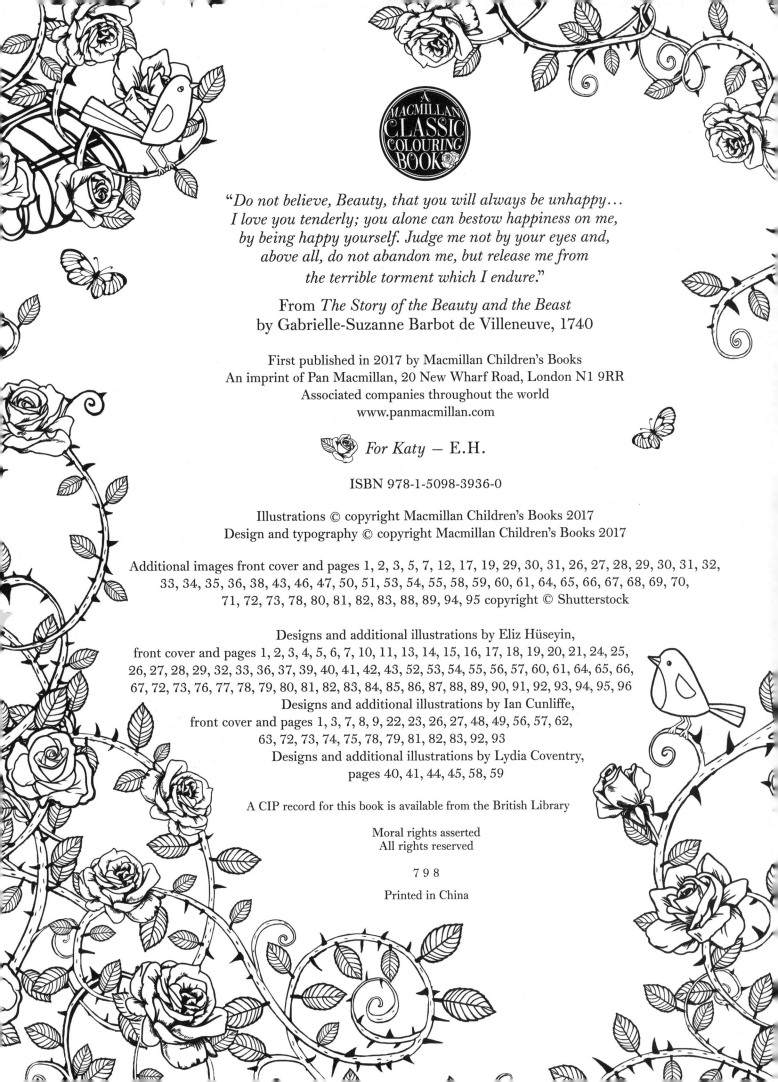

A MACMILLAN CLASSIC COLOURING BOOK

"Do not believe, Beauty, that you will always be unhappy…
I love you tenderly; you alone can bestow happiness on me,
by being happy yourself. Judge me not by your eyes and,
above all, do not abandon me, but release me from
the terrible torment which I endure."

From *The Story of the Beauty and the Beast*
by Gabrielle-Suzanne Barbot de Villeneuve, 1740

First published in 2017 by Macmillan Children's Books
An imprint of Pan Macmillan, 20 New Wharf Road, London N1 9RR
Associated companies throughout the world
www.panmacmillan.com

For Katy — E.H.

ISBN 978-1-5098-3936-0

Illustrations © copyright Macmillan Children's Books 2017
Design and typography © copyright Macmillan Children's Books 2017

Additional images front cover and pages 1, 2, 3, 5, 7, 12, 17, 19, 29, 30, 31, 26, 27, 28, 29, 30, 31, 32, 33, 34, 35, 36, 38, 43, 46, 47, 50, 51, 53, 54, 55, 58, 59, 60, 61, 64, 65, 66, 67, 68, 69, 70, 71, 72, 73, 78, 80, 81, 82, 83, 88, 89, 94, 95 copyright © Shutterstock

Designs and additional illustrations by Eliz Hüseyin,
front cover and pages 1, 2, 3, 4, 5, 6, 7, 10, 11, 13, 14, 15, 16, 17, 18, 19, 20, 21, 24, 25, 26, 27, 28, 29, 32, 33, 36, 37, 39, 40, 41, 42, 43, 52, 53, 54, 55, 56, 57, 60, 61, 64, 65, 66, 67, 72, 73, 76, 77, 78, 79, 80, 81, 82, 83, 84, 85, 86, 87, 88, 89, 90, 91, 92, 93, 94, 95, 96
Designs and additional illustrations by Ian Cunliffe,
front cover and pages 1, 3, 7, 8, 9, 22, 23, 26, 27, 48, 49, 56, 57, 62, 63, 72, 73, 74, 75, 78, 79, 81, 82, 83, 92, 93
Designs and additional illustrations by Lydia Coventry,
pages 40, 41, 44, 45, 58, 59

A CIP record for this book is available from the British Library

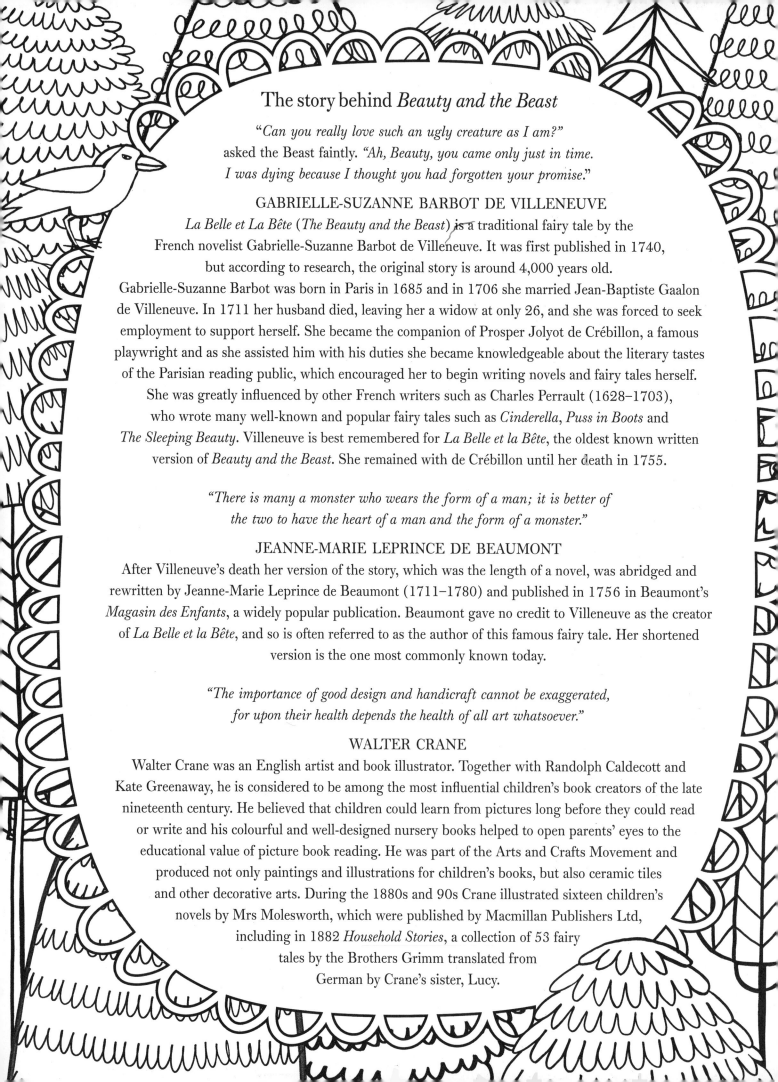

The story behind *Beauty and the Beast*

"Can you really love such an ugly creature as I am?"
asked the Beast faintly. *"Ah, Beauty, you came only just in time.
I was dying because I thought you had forgotten your promise."*

GABRIELLE-SUZANNE BARBOT DE VILLENEUVE

La Belle et La Bête (*The Beauty and the Beast*) is a traditional fairy tale by the
French novelist Gabrielle-Suzanne Barbot de Villeneuve. It was first published in 1740,
but according to research, the original story is around 4,000 years old.
Gabrielle-Suzanne Barbot was born in Paris in 1685 and in 1706 she married Jean-Baptiste Gaalon
de Villeneuve. In 1711 her husband died, leaving her a widow at only 26, and she was forced to seek
employment to support herself. She became the companion of Prosper Jolyot de Crébillon, a famous
playwright and as she assisted him with his duties she became knowledgeable about the literary tastes
of the Parisian reading public, which encouraged her to begin writing novels and fairy tales herself.
She was greatly influenced by other French writers such as Charles Perrault (1628–1703),
who wrote many well-known and popular fairy tales such as *Cinderella*, *Puss in Boots* and
The Sleeping Beauty. Villeneuve is best remembered for *La Belle et la Bête*, the oldest known written
version of *Beauty and the Beast*. She remained with de Crébillon until her death in 1755.

*"There is many a monster who wears the form of a man; it is better of
the two to have the heart of a man and the form of a monster."*

JEANNE-MARIE LEPRINCE DE BEAUMONT

After Villeneuve's death her version of the story, which was the length of a novel, was abridged and
rewritten by Jeanne-Marie Leprince de Beaumont (1711–1780) and published in 1756 in Beaumont's
Magasin des Enfants, a widely popular publication. Beaumont gave no credit to Villeneuve as the creator
of *La Belle et la Bête*, and so is often referred to as the author of this famous fairy tale. Her shortened
version is the one most commonly known today.

*"The importance of good design and handicraft cannot be exaggerated,
for upon their health depends the health of all art whatsoever."*

WALTER CRANE

Walter Crane was an English artist and book illustrator. Together with Randolph Caldecott and
Kate Greenaway, he is considered to be among the most influential children's book creators of the late
nineteenth century. He believed that children could learn from pictures long before they could read
or write and his colourful and well-designed nursery books helped to open parents' eyes to the
educational value of picture book reading. He was part of the Arts and Crafts Movement and
produced not only paintings and illustrations for children's books, but also ceramic tiles
and other decorative arts. During the 1880s and 90s Crane illustrated sixteen children's
novels by Mrs Molesworth, which were published by Macmillan Publishers Ltd,
including in 1882 *Household Stories*, a collection of 53 fairy
tales by the Brothers Grimm translated from
German by Crane's sister, Lucy.